Sybil Rides
for
Independence
by Drollene P. Brown
with pictures by Margot Apple

Albert Whitman & Company, Niles, Illinois

To ~ Shauna Tittle and Mark Tittle D.B.
Christine North and Dakota and Marcy Edwards M.A.

Library of Congress Cataloging in Publication Data

Brown, Drollene P.
   Sybil rides for independence.

   Summary: Describes sixteen-year-old Sybil Ludington's
dangerous ride in 1777 to warn the minutemen of the British
attack on Danbury, Connecticut.
   1. Ludington, Sybil, b. 1761—Juvenile literature.
2. Danbury (Conn.)—Burning by the British, 1777—Biography
—Juvenile literature. 3. Danbury (Conn.)—Burning by the
British, 1777—Juvenile literature. [1. Ludington, Sybil,
b. 1761. 2. Danbury (Conn.)—Burning by the British, 1777
—Biography. 3. United States—History—Revolution, 1775–
1783—Biography]   I. Apple, Margot. ill.   II. Title.
E241.D2L833   1985   973.3'33   [92]   84-17219 ISBN
0-8075-7684-0

The text of this book is set in fourteen-point Caslon 540.

Text © 1985 by Drollene P. Brown
Illustrations © 1985 by Margot Apple
Published in 1985 by Albert Whitman & Company, Niles, Illinois
Published simultaneously in Canada by General Publishing, Limited, Toronto
All rights reserved. Printed in the United States of America
10   9   8   7   6   5   4   3   2   1

Contents

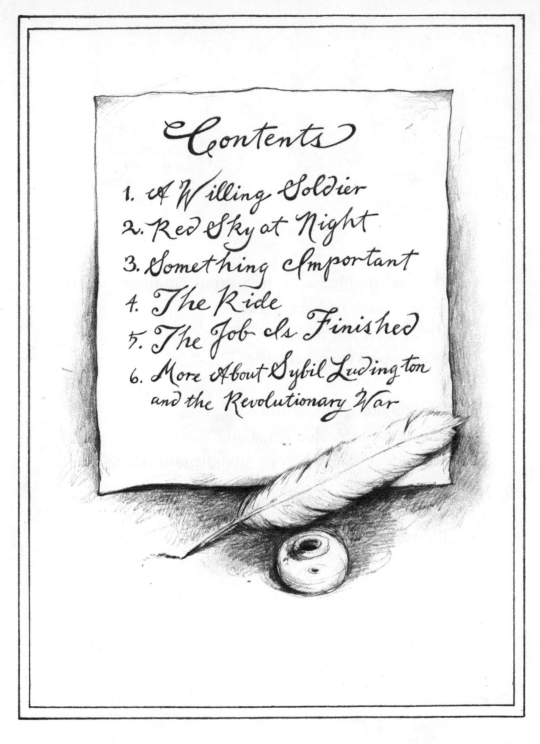

A Willing Soldier

Hooves thudded into the yard at Ludingtons' Mills,
in the colony of New York.
A red-faced girl reined in her horse
and jumped from his back.

"You're late again, Sybil,"
nine-year-old Archie declared.
"Mother wants you to go straight into the house."

Sybil sighed.
She handed the reins to Archie
and went in to face their mother.

"I know your father told you
to exercise Star every day," Mother scolded.
"But you must still do your chores.
Rebecca did your work today."

"I'm sorry, Rebecca," Sybil said.
"I lost track of time.
I was dreaming of riding with Father's regiment.
Oh, I wish I could be a soldier for the colonies!"

Mother shook her head.
"When I was sixteen, you were already one year old.
I took care of you and kept house.
Now you are sixteen, Sybil.
It is time to act like a woman.
Your duty is at home,
baking bread, mending clothes, washing dishes."

As Mother went upstairs, Rebecca spoke softly.
"I don't like washing dishes," she murmured,
"but I don't want to be a soldier."

"I'm not trying to avoid chores!" Sybil exclaimed.
"But I don't wish to be ruled by the king of England.
I want to help our army defeat the British
so the colonies can be free and independent."

"We do help," Rebecca said proudly.
"Our father is Henry Ludington.
He commands the only colonial regiment for miles around.
We help him."

"I know that," Sybil declared.
"But I want to do more than carry food and bedding
to those who spy against the British and hide in our barn.
I want to do something that is brave."

Something happened
on the night of April 26, 1777.
On that night, a weary rider reached the yard.
He brought a message for Colonel Ludington.

The rider pointed to the east.
The sky was red.
"Danbury's burning!" he shouted.

Archie ran out to care for the man's horse.
His eyes grew wide when he heard the next words.

"The Redcoats landed at Fairfield yesterday
and marched the twenty-three miles to Danbury.
There was no one along the way to stop them.
They reached Danbury at three o'clock today
and set fire to our houses and the army's supplies."

Colonel Ludington frowned.
"General Washington is in Peekskill," he said.
"But it would take him two days to get to Danbury.
My men could be there tomorrow morning.
It's up to us to stop the British!"

The colonel paced back and forth in the yard.
"I'll stay here to make the battle plans.
Someone must go to the villages and farms
to tell my men we have to march."

"I can do it," said the messenger.
"Lend me a fresh horse."

"No, my friend," answered the colonel.
"You must rest. You've ridden many hours.
I know someone who can do the job."

He led the soldier to the house,
then called to Archie.
"Son, put a saddle on Star!"

The men went into the warm kitchen.
The tired messenger sat down.
"Rebecca, dish up some food
for our weary friend," ordered the colonel.
"And Sybil, get the little ones ready for bed."

"Yes, Father," sang Rebecca.
She was happy she could watch the stranger.

"Yes, Father," answered Sybil with a sigh.
She would rather stay downstairs, too,
and hear what was happening.
Just her luck to be the oldest, she thought.

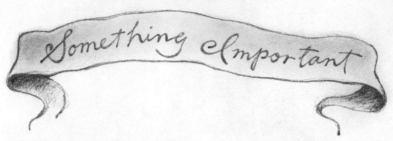

Something Important

Colonel Henry Ludington spoke quietly to his wife.
"Abigail, Sybil can handle Star
better than anyone else.
She trained that horse,
and she knows the whole territory."

"I know that," Sybil's mother replied.
"But if Redcoats see her,
they will stop her any way they can.
And there are 'skinners,' outlaws who steal
from the British and from us.
They may try to take Star.
Sybil will be in danger."

"All colonists who oppose the king of England
are in danger," the colonel answered.

His wife nodded. She called their daughter.
"Sybil, come down, please."

"Sybil is telling us a story!"
a tiny voice called back.

"Someone else can finish that," said Father.
"Your sister has something important to do."

Sybil ran down the stairs.
"What is it, Father?" she asked.

"The British have burned Danbury," Father explained.
"We must stop them before they do more harm.
But our men went home to care for their farms and
families after the last battle.
Someone must tell them it is time to fight again."

Sybil could feel her heart beating.
"Star and I will go," she said.

Bursting into the room, Archie heard his sister's words.
"It's already past seven," he objected.
"And Sybil, the night is cold and wet."

"And she's just a girl!" exclaimed the messenger,
looking at Colonel Ludington.

"She knows where all our men live," answered Father.
"Sybil has often ridden with me to their homes."

"But not at night," said Rebecca,
"and never when there were Redcoats around."

"Hush! Hush, all of you!" Mother commanded.
She put her own cape over Sybil's head and shoulders.
"This will keep you warm and dry.
Be careful, my daughter."

"Don't worry," Sybil said.
"Star is sure-footed.
He'll take care of me."

"Star knows about mud and stones," Mother replied,
"but he doesn't know about Redcoats or skinners.
You must also take care of Star."

Sybil felt a knot of fear in her stomach,
but she said nothing.
She kissed her mother,
waved to Rebecca and Archie,
and followed her father outside.

The Ride

Sybil swung up on Star.
She patted his neck and leaned toward his ear.
"This ride is for freedom," she whispered.

The colonel looked up at his daughter.
He handed her a big stick.
"Listen for others on the path," he warned.
"Pull off and hide if you hear hoofbeats
or footsteps or voices.

"You know where to go.
Tell our men that Danbury's burning.
Tell them to gather at Ludingtons'."
Sybil listened to her orders.
She saluted her father, her colonel.
He stepped back and returned the salute.

Sybil thought of what might happen.
There were more than thirty miles to cover
in the dark and rain.
She could be lost or hurt or caught by Redcoats!
But she did not let these black thoughts scare her.
I will do it for the colonies, she vowed.

She turned Star south on a line with the river.
There would be several lone farmhouses to alert
before they reached Shaw's Pond.

It was almost eight o'clock
when she reached the first farmhouse.
Doors flew open at the sound of Star's hoofbeats.

Sybil shouted her message. She did not stop,
but hurried on to the farmhouses
along Horse Pound Road.

It was about ten o'clock
when Sybil reached Shaw's Pond.
The houses beside the water
were dark for the night.

Sybil hadn't thought of this.
She had been so excited
she had forgotten people would be sleeping.

Sybil stopped for only a moment.
She coaxed Star up to the door
and pounded with her stick.

A window opened.
A head poked out.
"Look to the east!" Sybil shouted.
"Danbury's burning! Gather at Ludingtons'!"

She did not beat on every door.
She did not shout at every house.
Neighbors called to each other;
and in the little hamlets along her way,
one of the first ones awakened
rushed out to ring the town bell.

When the alarm began to sound,
Sybil would stop her shouting
and ride on into the darkness.

Her throat hurt from calling out her message.
Her heart beat wildly, and her tired eyes burned.
Her skirt seemed to be filled with heavy weights,
for it was wet and caked with mud.
She pulled her mother's cloak closer
against the cold and rain that would not stop.

Sybil would not stop, either.
All the men in the regiment must be told.
She urged Star on.

Outside the village at Mahopac Pond,
Star slipped in the mud.
He got up right away,
but Sybil's eyes stung with tears.
She would have to be more careful!

If Star were hurt, she would blame herself.
She must walk Star over loose rocks
and pick through the underbrush
where there was no path.

Again and again, Sybil woke up sleeping soldiers.
Nearing Red Mills, Star stumbled and almost fell.
He was breathing heavily.
"You are fine, Star," Sybil whispered.

Sybil looked at the sky.
The moon was half-risen.
That meant it was well past midnight.
She guessed they were halfway through,
but the long ride to Stormville still lay ahead.

More slowly now, they started on their way.
Then—hoofbeats on the path!
Quickly Sybil reined Star to a halt.
She jumped down and pulled him toward the trees.

She held her breath and strained her eyes.
Men passed so close she could have touched them.
They looked like British soldiers,
but sometimes skinners dressed like soldiers
of one army or the other
to fool the people they robbed.

Soon the hoofbeats died away.
Sybil's hands and knees trembled
as she guided Star back to the path.
"We'll make it," she softly promised him.
Star pricked up his ears and started off again.
He was weary, but he trusted Sybil.

When they reached Stormville,
the alarm had already begun to sound.
Someone from another village had come with the news.
Sybil was glad, for she could only whisper.
She had shouted away her voice.

Covered with mud,
Horse and rider turned home.

The Job Is Finished

When Sybil rode into her yard,
more than four hundred men were ready to march.
She looked at the eastern sky.
It was red.

"Is Danbury still burning?" she asked
and tumbled into Father's arms.

"No, my brave soldier.
It is the sunrise.
You have ridden all night."

"I do not feel like a brave soldier," Sybil whispered.
"I feel like a very tired girl.
Star needs care," she murmured sleepily
as she was carried to her bed.

Early that morning,
while that very tired girl slept,
her father's men joined soldiers from Connecticut.
They met the British at Ridgefield,
about ten miles from Danbury.

The soldiers from New York and Connecticut
battled with the Redcoats.
Most of the British escaped to their ships
in Long Island Sound,
but they did no further damage.

People spread the word of Sybil's ride.
Soon General Washington came to her house
to thank her for her courage.
Statesman Alexander Hamilton wrote to her,
praising her deed.

America was soon a growing, changing nation,
and Sybil's life changed, too.
At twenty-three she married Edmond Ogden.
They had six children, and she kept house.
She baked, she mended, and she washed the dishes.

But sometimes she would stop
in the middle of a chore.
Remembering that cold, wet night in 1777,
she would shiver again.
Then warm feelings of pride would fill her
as she thought, "Once I was brave for my country."

Sybil lived to be seventy-eight years old.
Her children and her children's children
loved to hear the story
of a young girl's ride for independence.

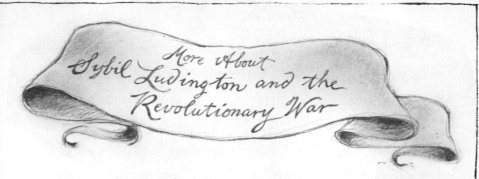

When the first American colonists arrived from England in the early 1660s, they thought of themselves as English, or British, citizens. But England was 3,000 miles away. The Americans had to solve problems on their own without help from their mother country, and over the years they became more and more independent of British control.

In 1763 the British began to tighten their rule over the colonies. They decided to station troops to protect the Americans from attacks by the French, Spanish, and Indians. The colonists were taxed to support these soldiers, and with each new tax, more colonists rebelled. The Boston Tea Party of 1773 was one of these protests. Outraged by a tax on tea, Boston citizens dressed as Indians boarded British ships and dumped their tea shipments into Boston Harbor. Soon England began to move the troops against its once loyal subjects.

On April 18, 1775, Paul Revere made his famous ride from Boston to tell people that the British were marching on the countryside. For several years before this, Revere had been riding, delivering news to the colonists. On this night he was captured by the Redcoats before he could finish his mission, but he was able to complete a very important job. He reached Lexington, Massachusetts, where he warned two Patriot leaders, John Hancock and Samuel Adams, that the British were coming. Dr. Samuel Prescott, captured with Revere, got away to warn the Minutemen between Lexington and Concord. (Minutemen were soldiers like Colonel Ludington's men. They did not stay in army camps but went home when there was no fighting. They promised to come back to fight "at a minute's notice.") On April 19, the Redcoats battled the Americans at Lexington and Concord, and the American Revolution began. It would last eight years.

Two years after Paul Revere's ride, Sybil set out on Star with news of Danbury's burning. By then many people thought the colonists were losing their fight, for Washington's army had been defeated many times. But six months later, there was an important American victory at the Battle of Saratoga. With news of this victory, Benjamin Franklin persuaded the French to enter the war on the side of the colonies. Later Spain and Holland also joined the conflict against England. After more years of fighting, England and America signed a peace treaty in 1783. The colonists had won their freedom from Britain.

Although Sybil Ludington was a real heroine of the American Revolution, we don't know too much about her. We do know that at the time of her ride, she had seven younger brothers and sisters. Four more were born after 1777. Sybil's mother was only fifteen years old when her first child was born! Such large families were common in those days, and an older girl like Sybil would have had many chores in the household. We can only imagine that she wanted to be a soldier; we can only guess what happened as she rode Star through the night to waken the Minutemen; but you can still trace her route. It is shown by historical markers around Ludingtonville, New York. You can also see a statue of Sybil on Star in Carmel, New York.

Some of the colonists—about one third—remained loyal to England. But most of them wanted to start their own country. Like Sybil, many did what they could to help. People who did not fight worked in other ways. They helped feed and clothe the soldiers, they spied against the British, and they carried messages. In those days, of course, you could not call someone on the telephone or announce something important on the radio or TV. Messages had to be carried on foot or by horseback, and this took a long time. (Sybil's ride took all night, but you could probably drive the same route in about an hour today.) When someone brought important news, bells were rung in the church steeple or the town square to gather the people.

Sybil's deed did not change the war, for the battle at Ridgefield was not significant. But the struggle for independence was won by the courage of people like Sybil and the Minutemen she warned.

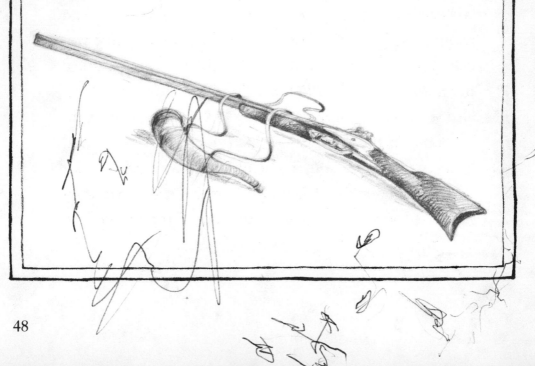